CELEBRATION STORIES
The
Best Prize of All

SAVIOUR PIROTTA

Illustrated by Sheena Dawson

HODDER
Wayland

an imprint of Hodder Children's Books

Celebrating Harvest

Harvest Festival is a time when Christians give thanks to God for the crops – the harvest – He has given them. It is an ancient tradition that started long before Christianity and takes place, in one form or another, in many countries around the world.

In some places, a festival is held. This might include a feast or a special dinner. Some communities celebrate Harvest with music and dancing. There are often competitions to show just how good the harvest has been.

In the past, Harvest was also a time for a community to store away food which would help it through the long, dark winter ahead. People then also asked God to look after their food store, to guard it from harm so that they might have enough to eat until the spring when new crops could be planted.

Harvest is a time for sharing, too. Many years ago, God ordered His people to look after the needy. In the Old Testament, we read: "When you harvest your fields, do not cut the corn to the edges of the fields; do not go back through your vineyard to gather the grapes that were missed; leave them for the poor people." So, during Harvest time, many Christians bring gifts to their churches or schools. The food is then distributed among those who need them.

The Giant Pumpkin

Linda stood at the bottom of the garden, a mug of hot tea in her hands.

"Are you checking that pumpkin again, pet?" asked Grandad, coming up behind her.

"I'm just making sure it's all right," said Linda. She looked at the giant pumpkin at her feet, its smooth skin pale and waxy.

"I must say we do seem to have a champion on our hands," said Grandad proudly. "It's all that manure we worked into the soil. And your constant watering, of course. Now, come on, you're going to be late for school."

Grandad headed towards the garage. He always drove Linda to school. Her parents, who were farmers, left the house at the crack of dawn.

Linda finished her tea and followed him. It was Friday, the day before the Harvest weekend, and she was looking forward to the special assembly at school.

But the real treat comes tomorrow, thought Linda as she climbed into Grandad's battered old car. That was when the Harvest Dinner would be held in the parish hall, followed by the annual Harvest competitions.

"When was the last time someone in our family won a prize at Harvest?" she asked her grandfather, tossing her bag on to the back seat.

"Your grandma, God rest her soul," said Grandad, "won the Tastiest Jam Or Preserve Of The Year Award in 1958. And I came second or third in the Strangest Fruit Or Vegetable Award category a couple of times."

"But no cups in the family since 1958," said Linda.

"No cups," Grandad agreed.

"Well, that's going to change this year," said Linda. "My pumpkin is going to win the Biggest Vegetable Of The Year Award, you'll see."

Grandad smiled but said nothing. He was concentrating on driving along the narrow, winding road. As they passed the gates of the disused army barracks at the edge of the village, Linda waved at a girl in a shapeless red dress and green wellies that came up to her knees.

The girl waved back shyly but did not smile. She was a refugee from Eastern Europe. Her family was staying in the barracks, along with some other refugees. For weeks, Linda had seen her standing by the gates, her big, dark eyes full of sadness. She seemed lonely and lost. Perhaps she was missing her friends back home, Linda thought.

"I wonder if they celebrate Harvest in that girl's country?" she said to Grandad as he stopped the car outside the school.

A Whispered Warning

The Harvest Assembly was taking longer than expected. The Headmaster was rambling on about how people had been celebrating Harvest festivals since the dawn of civilization. Linda wondered what the Headmaster meant by the 'dawn of civilization'. Had some people woken up one morning to find themselves changed overnight from savages into cultured people, complete with flowing robes and poems on the brain?

Fred Wakely, who was sitting in the row behind Linda, poked her in the back.

"Your precious pumpkin still doing fine?" he whispered.

Linda did not reply. Fred was just as determined to win the Biggest Vegetable Award as she was. Indeed, his family had won that particular prize for the past eight years.

"I'd keep on eye on it, if I were you," continued Fred, taunting her. "You never know what might happen to prize vegetables when they're left unattended."

"You leave my pumpkin alone, Fred Wakely!" hissed Linda under her breath.

Just then the Headmaster brought his talk to an end by saying that Harvest was a time to thank God for all his blessings. Everyone stood up and sang a Harvest hymn. Then Year 5 performed a play. It was very good – the script even had jokes in it. But Linda didn't enjoy it. She was far too worried about her pumpkin.

What if someone from Fred's family sneaked into the garden and smashed it while she was at school?

A Thief in the Night

"Why the long face, pet?" said Linda's mum, putting supper on the kitchen table. "Did you have a bad day at school?"

"Linda's convinced that the Wakelys are going to harm her giant pumpkin before the Harvest competition tomorrow," said Grandad, pouring out the tea.

"Don't be silly, pet," said Linda's dad. "No one's going to touch your pumpkin."

Linda wanted very much to believe him, but she couldn't. After tea, she went straight up to her room. It was already dark and Linda could hardly see anything out of the bedroom window. She wished the moon would come out so she could keep an eye on her pumpkin.

Linda turned on her cassette player and brought her chair close to the window. That way, if Fred Wakely tried any funny business, she'd spot him climbing over the fence. No one was going to steal her chance of winning a cup.

At bedtime, Mum brought Linda a cup of cocoa. "Good-night, love," she said, turning off the cassette player. "Don't forget to brush your teeth before you go to bed."

Linda nodded. She was tired, but she was determined not to fall asleep. She drank her cocoa, brushed her teeth in the bathroom and returned to her seat by the window.

After a while she heard her father snoring in the room next to hers. The clock in the hall downstairs ticked loudly: *tick, tock, tick, tock…*

Linda woke up with a start. She'd fallen asleep. For a moment she wondered why she wasn't in bed. Then she remembered. *The pumpkin!*

She looked out of the window. There was someone in the garden, trampling through the flowers – a tall figure in a dark jacket.

Linda struggled to open the window. "*Stop, thief!*" she yelled, her voice thick with panic and anger. But it was no use. A moment later, the startled burglar had climbed over the garden fence and was gone, taking Linda's pumpkin with him.

The Suspect

Linda was devastated. She was sitting in the parish hall, surrounded by people from the village, but she felt as if she was all alone. She could have been sitting on an iceberg at the North Pole for all she cared.

"Have something to eat, love," said Grandad, nudging her gently.

Linda shook her head. The table was groaning with delicious food but she couldn't eat a thing.

21

"Perhaps you'll win next year," said Mum.

Linda held back her tears. Who cared about next year? She wanted to win today, now, this evening.

"I'll get that Fred," she muttered, glaring at the Wakelys who were stuffing their mouths with ham pie at a table nearby.

"We have no proof that young Fred was the one who stole your pumpkin, love," said Linda's dad. "It could have been anyone."

Linda snorted. Not Fred indeed! Oh, Fred Wakely had certainly *denied* stealing the pumpkin. And it was true that Linda hadn't actually been able to see the thief's face… But Linda knew it was Fred – it had to be. He had resorted to cheating because he was afraid of losing a competition that his family had won for years.

The meal finished and the tables were cleared. Now the judges were ready to announce the winners of the competitions. Linda looked at the prize vegetables assembled on a long trestle table at one end of the parish hall. None of them were as big or as beautiful as her stolen pumpkin.

"I can't bear this any longer," she whispered to Grandad.

The old man slipped his hand into hers. "Come on, pet," he said. "Let's go home. I could do with a walk anyway."

The two of them slipped out of the hall, leaving Mum and Dad to enjoy the rest of the evening. The moon was shining brightly as they walked home slowly along the country lane.

"I wish the moon had been this bright last night," said Linda bitterly. "Then I would have caught Fred red-handed."

Grandad put his arm around Linda's shoulder.
"Let it go, love. These things happen. Next year
we'll grow another pumpkin – even bigger than
this year's. And I'll get us a greenhouse, so we
can lock it up where no one can touch it."

Linda and Grandad walked the rest of the
way in silence, both of them lost in their own
thoughts. As they passed the army barracks
Linda wondered about the girl with the red dress
and the sad eyes. Had she gone to bed? Was she
smiling in her dreams? Or did she never smile
at all?

"You all right?" asked Grandad.

"I guess so," Linda replied. They were close to home now. Linda could see the porch light shining in the dark.

Suddenly, Grandad stopped walking. He'd spotted something on the doorstep. "I don't believe it," he said, "It's your pumpkin, Linda. The thief has returned it."

An Apology

Linda was puzzled. Surely Fred wouldn't have had time to return her pumpkin? He was still at the parish hall, no doubt gloating over the shiny cup for Biggest Vegetable Of The Year Award.

Had he got someone else to do it?

The sound of the doorbell made Linda jump.

Grandad opened the door, squinting in the porch light. There were three people on the doorstep: a thin woman in a black dress, a tall lad with short hair – and the little girl in the red dress.

"Hello," said Linda to the girl.

The girl waved timidly.

The woman pushed the boy forward. "We sorry to bother you, mister," she said to Grandad. "My son, Skodo, has apology to make."

"I'm sorry I stole pumpkin," mumbled the lad.

"Oh," said Grandad, opening the door wider. "Well, I suppose you'd better all come in."

"Sorry we cause trouble," said the woman again. "My Skodo very naughty. I tell him is not right to steal other people's food, even in rich country like this. He says we must have pumpkin. You see, this weekend is Harvest back in our country. People make pumpkin fritters with sugar and honey. Skodo's sister, Anya, wants sweet fritters for Harvest. She say they remind her of home. But we have no pumpkins. That's why Skodo steal."

So Fred Wakely had not stolen Linda's pumpkin after all. She had been wrong to accuse him. And the real thief hadn't stolen the pumpkin for himself, either. He'd taken it for his little sister, the girl with the sad eyes who never smiled.

Linda looked at Anya. She seemed so fragile in her red dress, so lost and far away from home. And all she wanted was a slice of fried pumpkin with sugar. Linda felt herself go red in the face. She had so much to be thankful for – a loving family, a good school, food, clothes, toys, books, a roof over her head. The list was endless, but she still wanted more – cups and awards, the admiration of her friends…

"Please keep the pumpkin for your Harvest celebration," she said to Anya's mother.

"We cannot—" the woman began to protest.

"Please," Linda begged her. "We have more vegetables than we need. We'd be honoured if you took it."

"I'm afraid giant pumpkins don't taste very good," smiled Grandad. "They're grown for size rather than flavour. But we'll give you some smaller pumpkins from the garden. They'll be delicious."

A Special Invitation

It was Sunday evening. Linda and her family were sitting round the kitchen table, drinking tea.

"…So Linda told the lady to take the pumpkin," said Grandad proudly. "Wasn't that nice of her?"

"It certainly was," said Dad, collecting mugs and putting them in the sink. "Hello," he added, peering through the kitchen window. "I think we've got company."

Linda rushed to the window. There was a battered old van pulling up outside the front door. Skodo jumped out of it and rang the bell.

"Good evening," he said politely when Linda answered the door. "You invited to Harvest celebration."

Linda looked surprised. "Today?"

"In my country we celebrate Harvest on Sunday," explained Skodo. "You all invited." He turned to Grandad and Linda's parents. "Come, everything ready."

"But we couldn't possibly intrude…" began Linda's mum.

Skodo smiled again, and Linda knew that they couldn't refuse. "Come on, Mum," she said. "Let's go."

A few minutes later, Skodo's van was leading Grandad's car along the road to the army barracks. As they parked, Linda could hear music coming from a barn. Someone was playing a violin. There were flickering lights everywhere: in the trees and on the window-sills. A twisting pattern of candles, set in glass jars on the ground, led to the barn door.

Anya came out to meet them. She'd swapped her red dress for a bright green one with lace around the collar, but she was still wearing her wellies. She gave Linda a garland of flowers to put round her neck.

Linda followed her towards the barn. As they went in, the music stopped. A crowd of people turned to stare at them. Then Skodo's mum stepped forward and said in a loud voice, "Thank you for coming, our special guests."

A murmur of approval went round the barn.
The music started again, and people began to
dance.

Linda found herself being pulled into a circle
of dancers.

Mum followed nervously, saying, "Oh, no,
I can't, I haven't danced for years…"

The Prizewinner's Cup

After everyone had danced around the barn, laughing and clapping, the violin player put down his instrument and started beating on a drum. A woman came through the door with a large wooden tray.

"Pumpkin fritters," Skodo said to Linda and
Grandad.

The woman started handing out the food.
She was followed by other grown-ups, with
wine for the adults and lemonade for the
children. Soon everyone was eating and
drinking, laughing and talking.

"Look at them," said Skodo proudly, beaming at the crowd. "They have all lost their homes. Many have even lost family. But tonight they celebrate. They thank God for all He has given them." He smiled at Linda. "To you, living in an old army barracks might not seem so good. But these people are grateful to be alive and safe. Many others have not been so lucky."

"Yes," sighed Linda, "we should always be thankful for what we have."

Someone gently tugged at Linda's sleeve. She turned to see Anya behind her, holding something covered by a chequered cloth.

"Excuse my sister," said Skodo. "She has not talked or smiled since our father was shot by the soldiers. She wants to give you a present. Something to make up for the prize you did not win yesterday."

"How do you know about that?" Linda asked, surprised.

Skodo laughed. "Oh, we know everything that goes on in the village…"

Gently, Linda slid the cloth away. Anya was holding a hollowed-out pumpkin. Someone had carved intricate designs in the skin, making it look like a precious cup.

Linda gasped. She had never seen anything so beautiful in all her life.

"A prizewinner's cup," laughed Grandad.

"We don't like to waste any part of the pumpkin," explained Skodo, "so we always use the skin. It will dry out and become hard, then you can drink out of it."

"It's perfect – much better than the prize I would have won for my pumpkin," said Linda, grinning and holding up the cup for everyone to see. "I'll put it on the shelf in my bedroom. That way I'll be able to see it every night before I go to bed."

She smiled at Anya. The little girl looked back at her proudly. And then, something truly wonderful happened. For the first time since Linda had seen her at the army barracks' gate, Anya smiled. And *that* was the best prize of all.

45

Glossary

Barracks A group of buildings used to house soldiers, or other people in the military forces.

Fritters Pieces of food that have been dipped in hot oil and fried.

Harvest A crop that is ripe for picking. In a religious sense, Harvest is also a festival held to thank God for his kindness.

Parish Hall A building where local people can meet for different activities.

Preserve A sort of jam made by cooking fruit or vegetables with sugar.

Refugees People who are forced to leave their home or country.

CELEBRATION STORIES

Look out for these other titles in the **Celebration Stories** series:

Coming Home by Jamila Gavin
It's almost Divali, and there's lots to do. But then Preeta goes missing – and in the world of the gods, a battle rages between good and evil. When the night grows dark, will the Divali candles light everyone safely home?

The Guru's Family by Pratima Mitchell
When Baljit visits the Panjab, he realizes that his family is scattered around the world – just like the stars in the night sky. So, when Guru Nanak's Birthday comes, Baljit and his cousin, Priti, use the Internet to bring everyone together.

The Taste of Winter by Adèle Geras
Naomi is going to talk about Hanukkah at her school's Winter Festivals Assembly. She needs something for the display – but what? Just when she thinks she's found the answer, a perfect solution comes from an unexpected place.

You can buy all these books from your local bookseller, or order them direct from the publisher. For more information about Celebration Stories, write to: *The Sales Department, Hodder Children's Books, a division of Hodder Headline Limited, 338 Euston Road, London NW1 3BH.*